Elliot's
Christmas Surprise

To Barbara Julie

Kids Can Press acknowledges the financial support of the Ontario Arts Council, the Canada Council for the Arts and the Government of Canada, through the BPIDP, for our publishing activity.

Published in Canada by
Kids Can Press Ltd.
29 Birch Avenue
Toronto, ON M4V 1E2

Published in the U.S. by
Kids Can Press Ltd.
2250 Military Road
Tonawanda, NY 14150

www.kidscanpress.com

The artwork in this book was rendered in pencil crayon. The text is set in Minion.

Edited by Debbie Rogosin
Designed by Karen Powers
Printed in Hong Kong, China, by Book Art Inc., Toronto

The hardcover edition of this book is smyth sewn casebound.
The paperback edition of this book is limp sewn with a drawn-on cover.

CM 03 0 9 8 7 6 5 4 3 2 1
CM PA 03 0 9 8 7 6 5 4 3 2 1

National Library of Canada Cataloguing in Publication Data

Beck, Andrea, 1956–
Elliot's Christmas surprise / written and illustrated by Andrea Beck.

"An Elliot Moose story."

ISBN 1-55337-474-6 (bound). ISBN 1-55337-661-7 (pbk.)

I. Title.

PS8553.E2948E446 2003 jC813'.54 C2002-905918-6
PZ7

Kids Can Press is a Corus™ Entertainment company

Elliot's Christmas Surprise

Written and Illustrated by

ANDREA BECK

KIDS CAN PRESS

North Pole
SANTA'S WORKSHOP

ELLIOT MOOSE was dreaming of Santa and the North Pole when a little noise tugged him awake. He opened his eyes and grinned from ear to ear.

"It's Christmas Eve!" he shouted. "Santa's coming *tonight!*"

Then Elliot saw something extraordinary.

There, at the end of Elliot's bed, was a gigantic red box! Elliot blinked. It was the very same red as Santa's suit!

"Santa came early!" he yelled. "It's a Special Delivery, because I've been extra good this year!"

Elliot scrambled to the doorway and peeked around the corner. What had Santa left for his friend Socks?

His grin faded.

Santa hadn't left her a thing.

Elliot was itching to open his box, but he didn't want Socks to feel left out.

"She needs a Special Delivery, too!" he decided. "Then we can open them together."

And so, even though he'd already made her a Christmas present, he drew a Best Friends picture and put it in a special frame. He wrapped it up, tied it with wool and placed it next to his box.

Elliot was about to call Socks when he remembered Paisley.

He didn't want Paisley to feel left out either.

So Elliot made him a fancy checkerboard, because Paisley loved games. He wrapped it up, gave it a bow and placed it next to his box.

Elliot was about to call Socks and Paisley when he remembered Amy.

He groaned. If he made an extra gift for Amy, then he should make one for Angel. And that meant extra gifts for Snowy, Puff, Beaverton and Lionel, too!

Getting a Special Delivery from Santa was turning out to be a lot of work.

Elliot got dressed. Then he settled down and made fairy wings for Snowy and a bug headband for Puff, a macaroni necklace for Amy and a Home Sweet Home sign for Lionel, a recipe box for Beaverton and a truck garage for Angel.

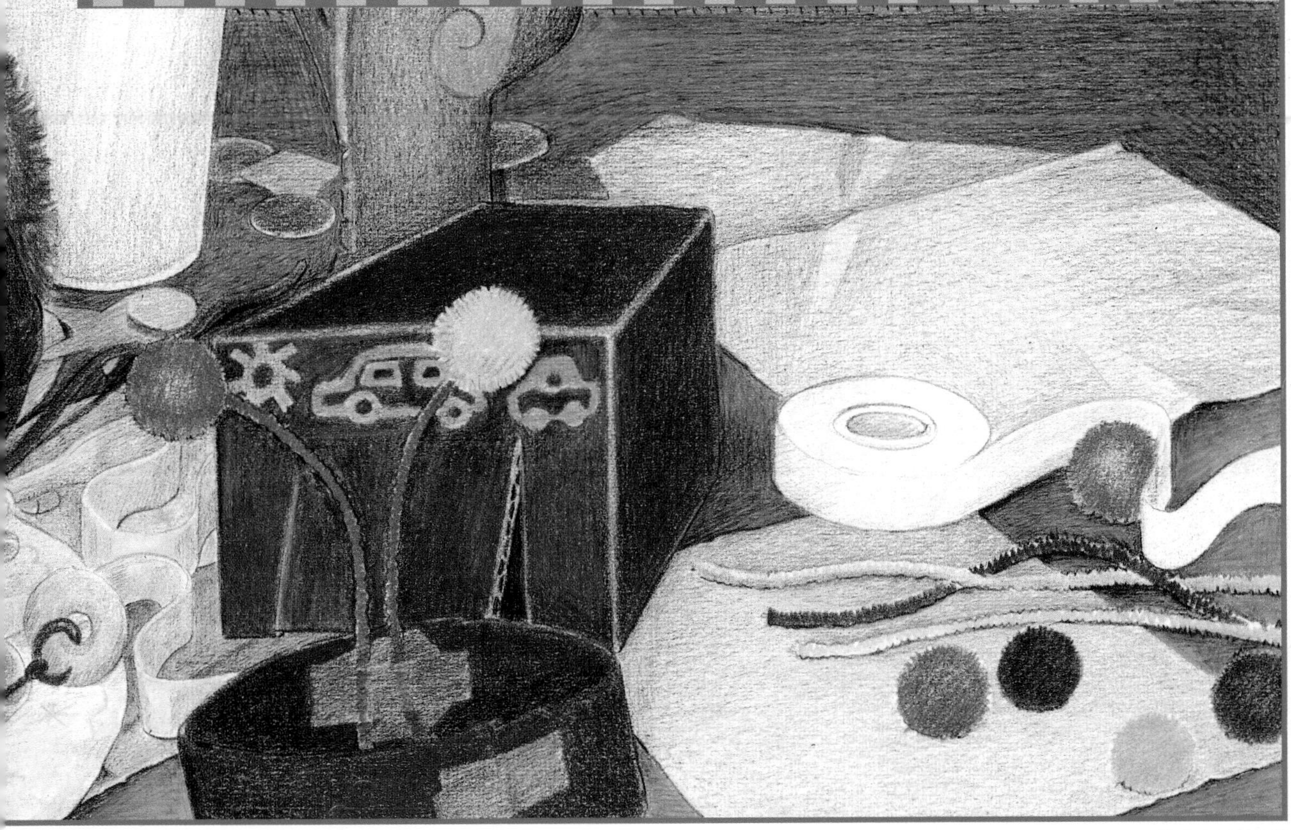

When the presents were done, Elliot wrapped them up, tied them with wool and placed them next to his box. He raced to the stairs and called up as loudly as he could, "Socks! Paisley! Everyone! I have surprises for you!"

Then Elliot half skipped, half ran back to his box.

What had Santa brought? A train set? A race-car track? It was definitely something big!

Elliot couldn't wait a moment longer.

He lifted the lid a crack and peered into the dark box.

He couldn't see a thing, so he felt around with his paw. Nothing! Frantically, Elliot threw off the lid and tipped the box upside down.

"Where's my present?" he wailed.

His Santa box was empty!

After a moment, Elliot noticed a letter on the floor. It said

Dear Elliot,
I know you love to make things.
I thought you might have fun with
this box while you wait for Santa!
Love,
Lionel

Elliot dropped the letter.
This wasn't a Special Delivery from Santa!
It was just some old box that Lionel had found.

Elliot slumped to the floor.

Santa hadn't thought he was extra good after all. And now everyone would have a present except him!

Elliot was holding back tears when Socks came rushing in.

"Presents!" she cried gleefully. "*Before* Christmas?"

"Yes," muttered Elliot. "A Special Delivery … from me."

Socks tore open her gift.
"Oh, Elliot!" she shrieked.
"I love it! Thank you."

Then she gave him a great big happy hug, and something surprising happened.

Elliot straightened up. He couldn't help but smile.

Socks liked his gift!

She *loved* it!

"You're welcome," he said, with a pleased little wriggle.

One by one, Elliot's other friends opened their gifts. And each time someone thanked him and gave him a hug, Elliot felt the same happy, wriggly feeling as before.

When all the gifts were opened, Socks asked about the big box.

"That was *my* surprise, from Lionel," said Elliot.

"Whoa! I wish I had a box like that!" said Puff.

Elliot grinned.

It was true. Big boxes were hard to find. And this one was huge. It *was* a present. A really good present.

Then Elliot remembered something important. He thanked Lionel and gave him a great big hug.

“Who wants to make a Santa sleigh?” shouted Elliot.

“Me!” everyone yelled at once.

They gathered ribbon for the reins, sticks for the runners and pillows for the seats. And as they cut and tied and decorated, the box grew into a glorious sleigh.

Laughing and singing, the friends pranced around the house all afternoon.

That night, after the stockings were hung, Elliot and Socks and all their friends scampered off to bed. It was Christmas Eve and Santa was on his way.